Crazy about
puppies?

S_____'s mum is a
cham___on sheepdog.
W_ll _tar follow in
he _pawsteps?

Want to know about real life
working dogs?

'Gill___ _ewis, a former vet, is a
major talent'
THE TIMES

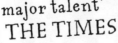

No sheep were
harmed in the _____
of thi_ _____

Welcome to Sausage Dreams **Puppy Academy**, where a team of plucky young pups are learning how to be all sorts of working dogs. Let's meet some of the students...

STAR

the speedy one!

BREED Border collie

SPECIAL SKILL
Sensing danger

Scout
THE SMART ONE!

BREED German shepherd

SPECIAL SKILL
Sniffing out crime

PiP
the FRiENDLY ONE!

BREED Labrador

SPECIAL SKILL
Ball games

MURPHY
the BiG ONE!

BREED Leonberger

SPECIAL SKILL
Swimming

MAJOR BONES

One of the teachers at the
Sausage Dreams **Puppy Academy**.
Known for being strict.

PROFESSOR OFFENBACH

Head of the Sausage Dreams **Puppy Academy**. She is a small dog with A VERY LOUD VOICE!

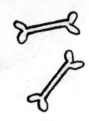

OXFORD
UNIVERSITY PRESS

Great Clarendon Street, Oxford OX2 6DP
Oxford University Press is a department of the University of Oxford.
It furthers the University's objective of excellence in research, scholarship,
and education by publishing worldwide in

Oxford   New York

Auckland Cape Town Dar es Salaam Hong Kong Karachi
Kuala Lumpur Madrid Melbourne Mexico City Nairobi
New Delhi Shanghai Taipei Toronto

With offices in

Argentina Austria Brazil Chile Czech Republic France Greece
Guatemala Hungary Italy Japan Poland Portugal Singapore
South Korea Switzerland Thailand Turkey Ukraine Vietnam

Oxford is a registered trade mark of Oxford University Press
in the UK and in certain other countries

British Library Cataloguing in Publication Data

Data available

ISBN: 978-0-19-273922-3

1 3 5 7 9 10 8 6 4 2

Printed in UK

Paper used in the production of this book is a natural,
recyclable product made from wood grown in sustainable forests
The manufacturing process conforms to the environmental
regulations of the country of origin

GILL Lewis
Puppy Academy

ILLUSTRATED BY
SARAH HORNE

STAR
ON STORMY MOUNTAIN

OXFORD
UNIVERSITY PRESS

1

The collie pups, Star, Gwen, Nevis, and Shep, pushed their way to the front of the crowd gathered at the bottom of the hill. A hushed silence fell across the dogs and humans. It was the final of the National Sheepdog Trials, and it looked like Bleak Tarn, the old gnarled collie and five times winner, was set to win again.

But there was one dog remaining. One dog who still had to run her turn.

Gwen nudged Star with her paw. 'Look, here comes your mum.'

The pups watched Star's mum, Lillabelle of Langdale Pike, trot alongside her shepherd. The black-and-white collie waited for the signal, and then she was off. She

raced up the hillside in a long curve towards the small flock of sheep grazing in the far field. She leapt the low wall and came behind the sheep, slowing down as she did so. She knew that if she ran in too fast she would scare them and they would scatter. The sheep saw her and tightened together. Lillabelle kept her head low and crept towards them, and the small flock set off steadily down the hillside towards the crowds.

'That's a perfect lift,' said Nevis.

'If the rest of the trial goes this well, your mum might win,' said Shep.

Lillabelle guided the sheep through narrow gates, and then drove them away into a circle marked on the ground. She had to single out the ewe with the green spot painted on her back. She circled the sheep, keeping them in a tight group, and when she saw the ewe on the outside of the flock, she swiftly trotted in and herded it away.

The crowd held its breath.

Maybe this was good enough to beat Bleak Tarn, but there was one last part of the trial to do. It was the most difficult part of all. Lillabelle had to herd the sheep into the square pen and shut the gate. It wouldn't be easy. The sheep were getting bored and restless. They wanted to be back out on the hillside with the rest of the flock.

Lillabelle kept them calm. If she charged in now, all would be lost. She tried to forget the crowds watching her. She tried to forget Bleak Tarn, who would be willing her to fail.

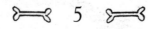

Keeping her belly low to the
ground, she crept forward. The
sheep bunched together more
tightly, looking for an escape route
to the hillside. But Lillabelle kept
them moving and, before they knew
it, the sheep had followed each
other into the pen. The shepherd

swung the gate shut and the crowd
exploded with applause.

She had done it. Bleak Tarn had
been beaten at last.

There was a new winner now.

A new champion.

Lillabelle of Langdale Pike had
won the National Sheepdog Trials.

Gwen turned to Star. 'Your mum is awesome,' she said.

'The best,' said Shep.

'My dad said she would win,' said Nevis.

Star puffed out her chest in pride. Her mum was a champion sheepdog. Everyone said Star would be a champion too. Star hoped so. She hoped one day she would win the National Sheepdog Trials and make her mum proud.

Star was looking forward to tomorrow. Tomorrow was the beginning of the pups' sheepdog training and Star couldn't wait to start.

❀

The next morning, Star, Gwen, Nevis, and Shep gathered in the classroom.

'Right,' said Major Bones. 'It's time to get started on your basic sheep-herding skills. We'll go out to the field and see if Hilda and Mabel are ready for us.'

The four collie pups followed Major Bones outside. Major Bones

was a teacher at the Sausage Dreams
Puppy Academy for Working Dogs.
There were all sorts of puppies at the
puppy academy. There were pups
that were training to be guide dogs,
pups that wanted to be hearing dogs,
and pups that wanted to be water
rescue dogs. But Star wanted to be
a sheepdog like her mum. She was

a Border collie, after all, and Border collies had sheep herding in their blood.

Hilda and Mabel, the academy sheep, weren't in the field. They were in the barn, sitting on a hay bale, nattering and knitting woollen blankets for dogs in rescue shelters.

'Ooh, hello, my dears,' Hilda bleated, seeing the collie pups.

'Hello,' baa-ed Mabel.

Hilda put her knitting down. 'Well, if it isn't little Gwen, Shep, Nevis, and Star,' she bleated. She gave Star a little wink. 'We're expecting great things from you.'

'Great things,' baa-ed Mabel in agreement.

Star smiled to herself. She imagined winning the National Sheepdog Trials: Star of Langdale Pike, the new champion.

'No need for idle chit-chat,' barked Major Bones. 'Let's get started.'

'Right-ho, right-ho,' bleated Hilda. 'Just give me time. My legs don't move so fast as they used to.'

'Not so fast,' baa-ed Mabel.

They climbed down from the hay bale and hobbled outside into the field.

Hilda and Mabel had lived at the puppy academy longer than anyone could remember and had taught many young collies the basics of herding sheep. They were gentle, kind, and patient sheep, although they could only manage a slow shuffle around the field.

'Now then, young 'uns,' said

Hilda. 'Mabel and I will stand over there.' She pointed to the far end of the field. 'And you have to run around us and drive us through that gate and into that pen there.'

'That pen there,' baa-ed Mabel.

'Remember,' said Hilda. 'Run a wide curve and keep it nice and steady.'

'Nice and steady,' baa-ed Mabel.

Star watched Hilda and Mabel hobble away across the field. She could feel excitement fizz right through her. She was about to herd sheep for the first time, ever. Her paws twitched. Her nose twitched.

Her muscles felt like coiled springs
just waiting to bounce.

Star was the last to take her turn.
She watched Gwen, and Nevis, and
Shep herd Hilda and Mabel across the
field and into the pen. Once or twice
Hilda pretended to hobble away, but
let the pups herd her back again.

All the time Star was watching them, she felt her muscles tighten even more. She wanted it to be her turn. She wanted to be herding Hilda and Mabel. Her heart thumped inside her chest. The tip of her tail tingled with excitement. She couldn't keep her feet still. She bounced up and down on the spot.

Major Bones waited for Hilda and Mabel to shuffle back to the far end of the field, and then he turned to Star. But before he could say GO, Star was off, streaking across the field in a blur of black-and-white fur. She leapt the fence, did a mid-air

half spin, and flew like a bullet towards
Hilda and Mabel.

'Oooh, heavens!' bleated Hilda,
breaking into a trot.

'Oh lordy!' baa-ed Mabel, running
off in a different direction.

Star ran around them to herd them
up again.

Lordy!

'Ooh, me knees,' bleated Hilda,
stumbling on a rock.

'Slow down, young 'un,' baa-ed
Mabel. 'We're not spring lambs any
more.'

But Star couldn't slow down. She was a sheepdog, and she had to herd these sheep. She ran round them in circles to keep them together. Round and round. Faster and faster. Round and round and round and round and round and round and round and round and round and round.

'Oooh! I'm quite dizzy,' bleated Hilda.

'My head's spinning,' baa-ed Mabel. 'I think I need a lie down.'

'Me too, dear,' agreed Hilda.

'STAR!' bellowed Major Bones. 'Come back at once.'

Star stopped running. She looked back at Major Bones, and then at Hilda and Mabel. What had she done? She hadn't even managed to herd them through the gates. She watched the two old ewes hobble back to the barn in giddy circles.

Gwen, Shep, and Nevis were just staring at her with their mouths wide open.

Star was supposed to be a sheepdog, the daughter of a champion, but her very first attempt at herding had gone horribly, horribly wrong.

2

'Too fast,' bleated Hilda.

'Much too faaaast,' baa-ed Mabel. 'You almost frightened the wool off my back.'

Star sat down next to the two sheep, who were lying in deep straw—recovering.

'I didn't mean to scare you,' said Star.

'We know that, my dear,' said Hilda, 'but other sheep won't. If you

go in so fast, they will think you're
going to attack them. You're not a
wolf, my dear. You are a Border collie
with sheep herding in your blood.
You've got to go in slowly and calmly.'

'Calmly,' repeated Mabel. 'I
remember your mum when she was a
young pup. Soft and gentle she was.
Paws like velvet.'

Star stared at her own
paws. They twitched

with energy. They wanted to be running, running, running. They wanted to jump and spring and bounce. How could she ever be like her mum? She had so much to live up to.

'Don't worry,' said Gwen at playtime. 'It'll be better next time, I'm sure.'

'But we won't be herding sheep,' said Nevis.

Star frowned. 'Why not?'

'The vet said Hilda and Mabel need a long rest after today.'

Shep pricked up his ears. 'What will we be herding?'

Nevis looked at them all. 'Haven't you heard? We'll be trying for our Level One Bo-Peep badge at the end of the week. And we won't be herding sheep. We'll be herding . . . ducks!'

'Ducks?' said Star.

'Ducks?' said Shep.

'Those quacky things?' said Gwen.

'Yes, ducks,' said Major Bones. 'Not exactly ideal, but they're the best we can do in the circumstances. I had a word with a few of the village ducks on the pond and they said they'd do it for a bag of grain.'

'But we're sheepdogs,' said Star, 'not duck-dogs!'

'A true Border collie can herd anything,' said Major Bones gruffly. 'Why, I remember the time your mother herded some human toddlers away from a busy road and back into a park.'

Star sighed. She looked enviously at Gwen, Nevis, and Shep. They

were never compared to anyone.
Sometimes she wished her mum
wasn't the National Sheepdog
Champion.

Star worried all week. The Level
One Bo-Peep badge was easy.
Everyone said so. In fact, no one had
failed it. But Star chased her tail in
worry. She wished Hilda and Mabel
would be there to help instead
of ducks. She'd never found the
village ducks particularly friendly.
They spent most of the time in the
water with their bottoms in the air,
ignoring everyone.

It was the end of the week. Friends
and family had arrived to watch the
pups take their Level One Bo-Peep
badge. Star had been practising
all week, running the course with
imaginary sheep. She saw her mum
and waved a paw. She wondered if
all the other parents expected Star to
be as brilliant as her own mum. She
wished there weren't so many people
watching.

'Quack!' said the ducks crossly.
'Quack...quack...quack...quack,
quack...'

The ducks gathered in an angry group in the middle of the field. Clearly they didn't want to be here. They had only come for the food.

'Quack...quack...quack... quack, quack...'

'**WELCOME,**' yapped Professor Offenbach.

Professor Offenbach was the head of the school. She was a small dog with a loud voice. Too loud, most people said, although no one dared tell Professor Offenbach that.

'WELCOME TO FRIENDS AND FAMILY ON THIS GLORIOUS AFTERNOON. TODAY IS A VERY SPECIAL DAY. OUR FOUR YOUNG PUPS WILL BE SHOWING THEIR DUCK . . . ER SHEEPDOG SKILLS. IN THE CROWD WE HAVE NONE OTHER THAN THE NATIONAL CHAMPION, LILLABELLE OF LANGDALE PIKE.'

A ripple of applause spread across the crowd.

Professor Offenbach glanced directly at Star. 'LET'S HOPE SOME OF THAT TALENT HAS RUBBED OFF ON A FEW OF OUR YOUNG PUPS TODAY.'

Star watched Gwen, Nevis, and
Shep take their turns. The ducks
were an awkward bunch, running
this way and that, quacking rudely
at everyone. But each of the pups

managed to coax them across the
field, through the gates, and into
the holding pen, where Major
Bones had scattered some grain to
encourage them in.

Star waited for her turn. Her
whole body trembled. Her paws

twitched. Her eyes focused on the rowdy ducks. They were dabbling in a puddle in the middle of the field, squabbling for the muddiest bit. *Go in slow on velvet feet*, Star told herself. But her body wasn't listening. Her feet wanted to run and run and run.

She was off, racing like a greyhound, her feet flying across the grass, her paws barely touching the ground. She leapt the gate with plenty of room to spare. Too high! Too fast! She went skidding and skittering towards the ducks. Round and round and round she spun.

BAM!

Feathers and mud flew into the air and Star landed with her face in the middle of the puddle.

She picked herself up. It hadn't been the greatest of starts, but she hadn't finished yet. Maybe she could still herd the ducks into the pen. Maybe she could still save face and earn her Level One Bo-Peep badge.

When the mud and feathers settled, Star looked around for the ducks. But they were nowhere to be seen. Nowhere at all. It was as if they had vanished into thin air.

Star looked up. High in the sky,

the ducks were getting smaller
and smaller and smaller as
they flapped away towards
the village.

Star felt everyone watching
her. She had nothing to herd
now. She wouldn't get her
Level One Bo-Peep badge.
She would be the first puppy
in the academy to fail
it. She couldn't face
any of the other pups.
She couldn't face her mum either.
Star scrambled up from the muddy
puddle and ran and ran and ran.

'Funny things, ducks,' bleated
Hilda.

'Temperamental,' agreed
Mabel.

'They flew away,' wailed
Star.

'It's their wings that does it,'
bleated Hilda.

'Wings!' baa-ed Mabel.

Star flumped down in the
straw. 'What was I meant to
do? Sprout wings too?'

'Star?'

Star looked up. Her mother
had found her hiding in the
barn with the sheep.

Star put her head in her paws. 'You're cross at me, aren't you? I've failed. I didn't pass the test.'

Lillabelle sat down next to her. 'Of course I'm not cross. It was only one test. It doesn't matter.'

'But I can't herd,' wailed Star. 'I'm too fast.'

'Too fast,' bleated Hilda.

'Like a rocket,' baa-ed Mabel. 'An out of control rocket,' she added as an afterthought.

'It's just excitement,' said Lillabelle. 'You'll learn.'

Star curled herself into a ball. 'But you never rushed in when you were young. I'll never be like you.'

'Star,' said Lillabelle softly. 'I don't want you to be like me. I want you to be you.'

'You mean fast and bouncy and can't keep still?' said Star crossly. 'Who wants a sheepdog like that?'

'You don't even have to be a sheepdog,' sighed Lillabelle. 'Just because I am, doesn't mean you have to be.'

'But what else can I be? I don't want to be a pampered pooch in the city. I want to be outside, running in the hills.'

Lillabelle put a paw on Star's shoulder. 'Star, you have many, many talents. One day you will find out what they're for.'

But Star wasn't listening. She had

covered her ears with her paws. She
was useless. She couldn't even herd
two old sheep or a few rowdy ducks.
What hope did she have herding a
huge flock of five hundred or more
sheep? She was no good at anything
at all.

3

'All aboard,' woofed Major Bones.

Star climbed into the minibus with the other collie pups.

Today they were heading off to Hilltop Farm in the mountains, to earn their Mountain Shepherd badge. They would be herding sheep down from the high hills.

Star sat next to Gwen and looked nervously out of the window. 'How many sheep do you think we will have to herd today?' she said.

'They have huge flocks in the mountains,' said Gwen.

'Oh,' said Star. 'I can't even herd a few ducks.'

'Don't worry,' said Gwen. 'You had a bad day the other day. Anyway, I heard Mabel say we don't have to herd the mountain sheep by ourselves. We'll do it as a team.'

'At least they won't have wings,' said Shep.

'We'll help each other,' said Nevis.

But Star was worried. The others seemed much better at herding than her. Would it really be that easy, working as a team?

The journey took a long, long time. Star hated having to sit still for so long. Her legs twitched with energy. After midday the minibus began to climb up towards the mountains. The roads became steeper and steeper and narrower and narrower. Green fields gave way to wide open mountain slopes of coarse stubby grass and trickling streams.

'Sheep,' said Gwen.

'Sheep,' said Nevis.

'Sheep,' said Shep.

They couldn't take their eyes from all the sheep. So many sheep.

They had never seen so many
together at one time.

But Star wasn't looking at the
sheep. She was looking up at the
mountains; at the way the clouds
swirled and danced across the
snow-capped peaks. She was looking
at the high ridges and the
tumbling waterfalls.

She was looking at the way the
sunlight played on the dark wet
rock. She wondered what it would
be like to run to the very top of the
mountains and feel the sun and the
wind in her fur. She wanted to be up
there; up in the clouds, higher than
the birds. She wanted to stand on
the very top of the world.

'Star,' said Gwen, giving her a poke.
Star pulled herself away from the
mountains.

'Look, there's Hilltop Farm,' said
Gwen.

In the distance, a white farmhouse
sat huddled at the base of the highest
mountain. Major Bones turned off the
main road onto the farm track. They
bounced and bumped, climbing higher
and higher, while the countryside

outside became wilder and wilder.

'Oh no,' said Nevis, shrinking back from the window.

'What?' said Shep.

'If I'm not mistaken, those are Herdwick sheep.'

'So?' said Gwen.

Nevis started to tremble. 'My dad told me that Herdwick are the toughest, meanest, and scariest sheep of all.'

Outside, the Herdwick sheep glared at them as they passed.

All the pups sank lower in their seats. They all wished Hilda and Mabel could be here instead.

'Welcome to Hilltop Farm.' An old
shaggy collie was waiting for them.
Thick dags of hardened mud clung to
the ends of his long fur and clunked
together like wind chimes in the
swirling wind. He had a greying
muzzle and an eyepatch across his
right eye. His left eye was as pale as
the winter sky.

'Good day, Angus,' said Major Bones, shaking his paw.

'Is it?' said Angus, casting his one eye up at the sky. 'There's snow in the air. I can feel it.'

Gwen looked up at the blue sky. There was hardly a cloud in sight. It didn't look like it was going to snow today.

'I know what you're thinking, wee lassie,' said Angus. 'But you're in the mountains now.' He paused, looking slowly at each of them. 'And mountains have their own ideas about the weather.'

The puppies huddled closer together.

 49

Angus lowered his voice as if he didn't want the hills to hear. He pointed to the craggy peak looming above them. 'And that there, is Stormy Mountain.'

'Stormy Mountain?' whispered Star.

'Aye,' said Angus. 'It lives up to its name. You wouldn't want to be up there when the clouds come down.'

Star felt a thin chill wind curl around her and ruffle her fur. She looked up at the mountain, towering above the farmhouse. Wisps of snow whipped up from the mountain top and swirled in the air. Deep down, Star knew Angus was right. She felt it in

her bones. She didn't know how she
knew, but she just knew a snowstorm
was coming.

'Well, let's get ye all to the barn
for a hot drink before we start,' said
Angus.

Star, Nevis, Shep, and Gwen
followed Major Bones and Angus
across the farmyard towards the barn.

'What's with the eyepatch?'
whispered Shep to Nevis.

Angus stopped. He turned around

slowly to look at them, fixing each of them with his pale eye.

'When I was a wee pup, laddie, I had a small disagreement with a ram,' he said. He lowered his voice. 'My advice to you is, watch out for the ones with horns.'

The pups looked nervously at each other. Shep's dad was right about Herdwick sheep. It seemed like they really were the toughest, meanest, scariest sheep of all.

4

In the short time it took to reach
the barn, the first few flurries of
snow began to fall.

'Now then,' said Angus. He
pointed to a map of the farm. 'For
your Mountain Shepherd badge, you
have to gather the sheep and their
lambs up here and herd them down
the hill, across the stream, down the
track, and into the farmyard here.
We'll be working as a team, but I
will be judging you individually.'

Gwen, Shep, and Nevis looked at the route Angus had shown them. But Star was looking at the footpaths and sheep tracks that crisscrossed the mountain. Some of the paths led to the very top.

'What about the rams?' said Shep.

'There'll be no rams in the flock today,' said Angus. 'But you'll have to keep an eye out for ramblers.'

'Ramblers?' said Star. She'd never heard of ramblers. 'Are they dangerous too?'

'No, wee lassie,' said Angus. 'Ramblers just get in the way sometimes, that's all. They're people who like to walk up the mountains.' He

pointed out through the barn doors
where a group of people in bright
waterproof coats and trousers, and
big leather boots, tromped across the
yard. They were carrying rucksacks
and maps, and the one in the front
was holding a compass.

'What do they do when they get
to the top?' asked Nevis.

'Well,' said Angus, 'they have a look around for a bit and then come back down again.'

Gwen frowned. 'What's the point in that?'

'Humans are crazy,' said Nevis. 'That's what my dad says.'

Star watched the people climb over the stile and head up into the hills. She didn't think they were crazy. She wanted to climb up the mountain too. She wanted to race across the high ridges and feel the wild wind in her fur. She wanted to see the whole world laid out before her.

A thin layer of snow coated the ground as they all made their way up the steep mountain track. The sheep and lambs were scattered across the hillside. Star tried to count them all. She reached two hundred but lost count. *Too many to count*, she thought. *How could Angus keep watch on them all?*

In a lower field, a ram with a scarred face and tattooed ear glared at them as they passed. Nevis stopped to look. He couldn't help staring at the ram's huge curly horns.

'Oi, fluff ball! What you looking at?' the ram baa-ed angrily.

Nevis hurried to catch up with the other pups, his tail between his legs. He hoped the ewes wouldn't be quite so scary. At least they didn't have horns.

Star watched the ramblers heading up Stormy Mountain. Some were in small groups. There were others walking alone. She counted ten people in all. People were easier to count than sheep. She secretly wished she could join them.

Angus led the pups across the hills to the lower slopes of the mountain. 'We'll need to bring all the sheep down today. There's bad weather on the way and the lambs might not survive the night if they're caught out here.'

Star looked up. Thick white clouds lay across the sky like a heavy duvet. Flakes of snow swirled down like feathers, covering the ground. Only the long spiky grasses showed through.

Angus sent the pups off in different directions to gather the sheep and bring them all together in one big flock. Star was sent out to the high slopes, to a stone wall separating the farm from the rest of the mountain. Star had been waiting to run all day. She had been cooped up in the minibus for too long and now her legs wanted to run and run. The sheep at the top were happily munching on lichens and moss. They didn't see Star coming. They didn't hear her feet racing across the ground, leaping from rock to rock, flying like a rocket towards them.

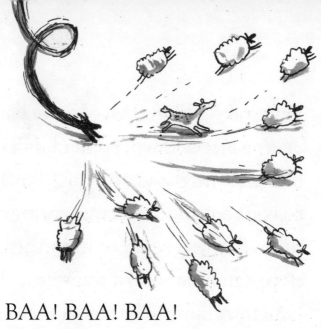

BAA! BAA! BAA!

BAA! BAA! BAA!

The lambs panicked. They scattered
in all directions, their mothers
galloping after them.

Oh no! thought Star. *I'm losing them.*
She ran faster in circles, round and
round them, but the lambs panicked
even more, scrambled over the wall,
and charged off up the hillside.

'YOUNG PUP!' An old ewe barred Star's way. She stamped her foot and snorted. She glared at Star. 'Just what do you think you're doing scaring the lambs like that? Do you want them to run off the edge of the mountain?'

Star sat down. She stared at her feet. Why did she have to be so fast? Why couldn't she remember to slow down?

Other sheep started to crowd around Star in a circle. 'It's no way for a

Border collie to behave,' baa-ed one.

'A disgrace,' baa-ed another.
'Leaping around like a wild thing.'

One ewe narrowed her eyes at Star.
'There's always a bad one . . . a wolf
in every pack.'

Star trembled as the angry flock of
sheep closed in around her.

'Ahem!' Angus pushed his way
through. 'Now ladies,' he said. 'Break
it up. Break it up. There's snow
coming. Let's gather up the lambs and
head down to the farm.'

The old ewe stamped her foot at
Angus.

'Please,' added Angus.

'That's better,' she said. 'Right girls, gather up your lambs. The old dog's right. Snows a-coming and we'd better tuck our young 'uns in the barn for the night.' She put her head in the air, ignoring Star, and trotted down the hillside with her lamb. The other sheep and lambs followed, glaring at Star with disgust.

Star looked up at Angus. She could see sympathy in his old face.

'Too fast, I know,' said Star. She turned and walked away, her head down and her tail between her legs.

The snow was falling faster now, building against the stone walls in thick drifts.

Angus caught up with her. 'I hope you don't mind,' he said, 'but I think it's better if you let the other pups bring the sheep down. It'll be dark soon enough, and we don't want to lose any lambs on the mountain tonight.'

Star nodded miserably. There was no way she could earn her Mountain Shepherd badge now.

5

Star stayed at the back of the flock
and watched as the other pups built
up their confidence, running this
way and that, keeping the sheep
together. She followed at a distance
as they came down from the hills,
across the stream, and joined
the ramblers returning from the
mountain. The weather was closing
in. No one, it seemed, wanted to be
stuck on the mountain tonight.

The sheep and lambs trotted into the warm light of the barn and began to munch on the sweet hay. Angus stood on the haystack and surveyed them all. 'Good job,' he said to Gwen, Nevis, and Shep. He looked out at the swirling snow in the darkening sky. 'We got them back home in time.'

Star knew they'd have to go back home to the academy soon too. She wouldn't get her Mountain Shepherd badge now. Maybe she would never be a sheepdog. She was walking towards the barn doors when an old ewe skittered past, bowling her over.

'BAA!' baa-ed the ewe. 'Laaaamb!'

'Lamb?' said Star.

The old ewe looked this way and that across the other sheep. 'I can't find my lamb. Laaamb!' she bleated across the barn. She ran to the doors. 'LAAAAAAMB!!' she bleated into the snowstorm. The wind whipped her bleat away, but there was no returning reply.

Angus looked worried. 'We must've lost one on the way down,' he said.

'Laaamb,' wailed the ewe.

Before anyone could stop her, Star was gone, racing out into the dark night, racing out into the storm. Her feet flew across the snow as she retraced the path. She leapt across the stream, circling and sniffing to find the lost lamb. Just beyond the stream, a set of tiny hoofprints left the path. They headed up, up, up, back towards the mountain. The hoofprints went round and round in circles. Star knew this lamb was lost and trying to find its way back home.

'Woof,' she barked. 'Woof!'

A muffled baa replied.

Star ran, pounding through the thick snow. If she didn't find the lamb soon the new snow would cover the prints and they would be lost forever.

At last, she found the lamb lying in a snowdrift, buried in snow, unable to climb out. The lamb was cold and wet through.

'Come on,' woofed Star. She put her nose underneath the lamb and pushed it out of the snowdrift.

The lamb struggled to its feet and wobbled after Star. Star waited for it, and together they made their way down the track.

The wind whirled around them. The lamb was weak, but Star gently nudged it down the hill. Sometimes the blizzard blew so fiercely that Star couldn't see her way at all, but she'd kept the map of the mountain in her head and found her way back down.

'Star, is that you?'

'BAAAA!'

Angus, Major Bones, and the old ewe were on their way up the track to meet them. The old ewe rushed over to her lamb.

'Well done,' said Angus. 'Your swift feet saved this young lamb.'

'Well done, indeed,' said Major Bones.

Star sighed. She was glad she'd saved the lamb, but she'd never be a true sheepdog if she couldn't control her feet.

Star followed them down the mountainside and joined the main track to the farmyard. The snow had stopped and a thin sliver of moon peeped through the clouds, lighting up the mountain tops. Star stopped to look. She had never seen anything so beautiful. The snow seemed to glow against the dark star-scattered sky. She wanted to be up there, racing beneath the moonlight across the powdery snow.

'Come on, Star, keep up,' woofed Major Bones.

Star turned and trotted down the track. Ramblers' footprints and sheep hoofprints all mixed together in the snow. The rubber soles of the ramblers' boots all left different prints. Star counted nine sets of prints coming down the mountain.

Nine!

She checked again.

She felt a knot of worry tighten in her chest. Her paws twitched.

There were only nine sets coming down, but Star remembered that ten people had gone up the mountain.

She looked back up at the towering peaks.

Someone hadn't returned.

Someone was still up there, on the mountain.

It was dark and cold, and another snowstorm was coming.

'Star!' Major Bones called again.

'Someone's stuck on Stormy Mountain,' Star called out.

'Star, come back.'

But it was too late. Star was already racing up and up and up the mountain path. Before Major Bones could call her name again, Star had disappeared into the velvet darkness of the night.

6

The path seemed to go on forever.
Star followed the cairns—the piles
of rocks left by walkers to show the
path. It was much colder up on the
mountain, and the wind blew through
her coat like sharp needles of ice.
Up and up and up she scrambled,
until she was on the very top of the
mountain. The whole of the world
was spread out before her.

The warm orange glow of the barn

light lay far, far below in the moonlit valley.

This was what it was like to stand at the very top of the world. Star wanted to stay longer, but she knew there wasn't time.

Star sniffed around the top of the mountain. She picked out lots of human scents, and then found one that headed away from the main path on its own. She followed it as it went round and round in circles,

like the lamb's hoofprints had. This
person was lost too.

Star followed the scent to a ridge
that led down the other side of the
mountain. But the trail continued
to the steep edge of the ridge, as
if someone had walked off the
mountain into thin air.

Star crept closer to the edge.
She looked over into the tumbling
darkness. On a thin ledge below her,
she could see a lumpy shape. The
shape groaned and moved.

It was a young man.

The lost rambler!

He must have fallen over the edge.

'Woof,' barked Star.

The rambler turned to look at her. Star could see he was hurt. His leg stuck out at a very odd angle. She scrambled down the rocks, leaping lightly across them.

'Woof,' she barked again. 'Woof.'

The man clung onto her. 'Good dog,' he said. 'Good dog.'

Star could feel his hands trembling. They were cold, so cold.

Star knew she wouldn't be able to help the man up. Even if he could walk, he wouldn't be able to climb back onto the ridge above. It was too high and too steep for him.

Star didn't know what to do. She wanted to tell him to wait and she'd find help, but she knew humans didn't understand her woofs and barks.

She couldn't leave the man alone. She sat beside him, trying to keep him warm, but his eyes kept closing. She knew that if he fell asleep he

might roll right off the narrow ledge.
She pawed at him and whined,
trying to keep him awake. But the
night was getting colder. Even with
her thick coat, Star could feel the
wind's icy fingers through her fur. Ice
crystals formed on her whiskers, and
her breath froze and sparkled in the
night air. Somehow she had to get the
rambler off the mountain, but how?
She knew for sure that he wouldn't
survive up here.

She stared out across the valley.
What could she do? Her wolf
ancestors would have howled across
the mountains to find each other.

Maybe that's what she should try. Star threw back her head and howled. She howled like the ancient wolf that was somewhere deep inside her. 'AAAAArrrrrOOOOOOOOOO! AAArrrrrOOOOOOOOOOOO!'

From far, far below came the baying of dogs, in reply.

It was Angus and Major Bones. They were coming up the mountain to find her.

AAROOOo

Major Bones and Angus were soon panting on the ridge above Star and the rambler.

Star bounded up the rocks to meet them, her paws light on the crumbly rocks.

'I think his leg is broken,' woofed Star.

Major Bones tried to climb down. He put a paw on one of the rocks, but the rock slipped under his weight and went tumbling and bouncing down into the darkness.

'We can't reach him,' woofed Major Bones.

'Too far down,' said Angus.

'We can't leave him,' said Star.

Major Bones pulled himself up to his full height. 'Right. Let's go back down to the farmhouse and get some help. We can't do this on our own.'

Angus nodded. 'I'll call Snowdon, he'll know what to do.'

'Snowdon?' said Star.

'Yes,' said Angus. 'Come on! We don't have much time.'

Star jumped back down onto the ledge. 'I'll stay with the rambler,' she said.

Major Bones looked at her. 'We can't leave you here too,' he said.

'Someone has to stay with him,'

said Star. 'Someone needs to keep
him warm and stop him falling
asleep, and I'm the only one who
can get down here.'

Major Bones didn't look happy,
but he agreed. 'Right,' he said.
'We'll be as fast as we can.'

Star huddled next to the rambler
to keep him warm.
It was even colder

now and it had begun to snow again. The clouds covered the moon, plunging them into deep, deep darkness. Every time the rambler drifted off into sleep, Star woofed to wake him.

Star wondered when help would come. She knew Major Bones and Angus wouldn't forget her, but it seemed so long since they had left to find help. She was cold and tired too, soooo tired. She knew she mustn't sleep, but maybe she could have a little nap. *Just a short one*, she told herself. She was drifting into sleep when she saw a light high up in the sky.

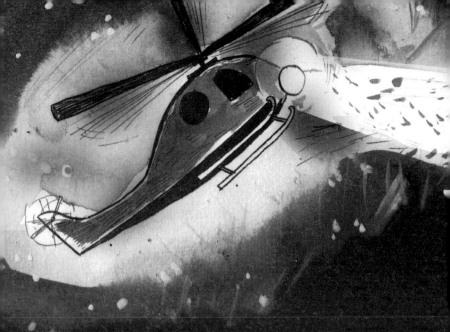

'Ducks?' she thought drowsily.
'Ducks with headlights?'

If they were ducks, they were
very noisy ducks, as if there were
hundreds of wings beating together
at once.

Star opened her eyes wide.
'Helicopter,' she woofed.
'Helicopter, helicopter, helicopter.'

The rambler rubbed his eyes.

'Helicopter,' Star barked again.

The helicopter's light was sweeping across the mountainside looking for them.

'Over here,' Star barked. But she knew the pilot wouldn't be able to hear them above the noise of the helicopter blades. She watched as

the helicopter swung away
and started to search another
part of the mountain. The
clouds were coming down again
and the wind was getting stronger.
The helicopter couldn't fly in thick
cloud. If it didn't find Star and the
rambler soon, it would have to leave
them on Stormy Mountain and
come back the next morning.

But the next morning might be
too late.

The rambler stirred. He fumbled
for something in his pocket. He
pulled out a small torch and
switched it on, but his hands were
so cold he couldn't hold

onto it. The torch slipped from
his fingers. Star watched it tumble
and bounce onto a narrower ledge
below, its light hidden by a rock.
She knew that if she climbed down
she might not be able to get back
up, but this might be their only
chance. Skittering down the slope,
she reached the torch and held it
up. She pointed its beam out into
the darkness, where it shone as
bright as any star.

The helicopter turned back and its light found Star and the rambler clinging to the mountain.

Star pressed herself against the rocks as the wind from the helicopter blades blew down on her. She watched a man drop down on a long wire and strap the rambler onto a stretcher.

'Come on, girl,' the rescuer said, holding out his arms to Star. 'We'll take you back with us too.'

Star clung to the man as the winch lifted them higher and higher, right into the helicopter.

'Well done, young 'un,' said a voice behind her.

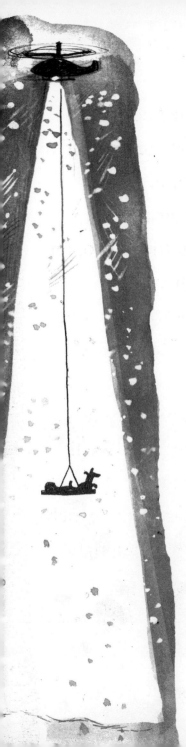

Star turned. A big Border collie wrapped a blanket around her. She couldn't help staring at him. What was a dog doing in the helicopter? The collie was wearing a bright-red reflective jacket of a type Star had never seen before.

'Who are you?' said Star, 'and what are you doing here?'

'I'm Snowdon,' said the collie. 'I'm with the Mountain Search and Rescue Team.'

7

All the puppies at the academy gathered together for the Friday award ceremony. Friends and family were there to watch too. Star sat right at the very back. She could see her mum looking for her, but she hid down behind Wolfie the wolfhound pup. She didn't want her mum to find out she hadn't earned her Mountain Shepherd badge.

Professor Offenbach climbed up onto the stage.

'WE HAVE QUITE A FEW AWARDS AND BADGES TO GET THROUGH TODAY,' she barked.

'FIRSTLY, I'D LIKE TO CALL WOLFIE UP FOR HIS ACTING PERFORMANCE AS THE WOLF IN THE VILLAGE PLAY OF LITTLE RED RIDING HOOD. EVERYONE SAID HE GOT INTO THE ROLE EXTREMELY WELL.' Professor Offenbach coughed. 'TOO WELL, A FEW VILLAGERS SAID. WE ONLY HOPE THEY WILL BE ABLE TO LEAVE THEIR HOMES AFTER DARK AGAIN SOON.'

Wolfie stood up to take his place on the giant sausage podium. Star glanced up to see her mum looking directly at her.

'AND NEXT,' bellowed Professor Offenbach, 'WE HAVE GWEN, NEVIS, AND SHEP, FOR ACHIEVING THEIR MOUNTAIN SHEPHERD BADGE.'

Star watched her friends gather on the podium. She wished she could be up there with them. She couldn't even look at her mother. She was the first Border collie in a long line of Border collies not good enough to be a sheepdog. She had failed. She half-listened to other pups collecting their awards and badges. Maybe she could slip out of the ceremony. She didn't want to stay any more.

'AND NOW . . . ' said Professor Offenbach, 'WE HAVE A NEW AWARD. IT HAS NEVER BEEN AWARDED TO ANY DOG AT THE ACADEMY BEFORE.'

Star crept along the back of the
hall and tried to sneak out.

'AND WE HAVE SOME SPECIAL
GUESTS TO AWARD IT.'

There was a commotion up at the
front, and Star could see humans,
dogs, and sheep coming through the
doors. It was Angus, and the old

ewe with her lamb, followed by
the rambler in a wheelchair, the
helicopter pilots, and Snowdon the
Mountain Rescue dog.

'I WOULD LIKE TO CALL STAR,
STAR OF LANGDALE PIKE, UP
ONTO THE PODIUM,' barked
Professor Offenbach.

Star looked around. Did she really
mean her?

'STAR, PLEASE COME TO THE PODIUM.'

For the first time in her life, Star's feet didn't want to move. They felt like they were stuck in thick, thick treacle.

Gwen was waving her paw at her. 'Come on, Star!'

'IN OUR FINE HISTORY AT THE ACADEMY, GUIDE DOGS, SHEEPDOGS, HEARING DOGS, AND MANY MORE HAVE PASSED OUT THROUGH OUR GATES,' woofed Professor Offenbach. 'BUT TODAY, WE HAVE A NEW AWARD TO HAND OUT.'

All eyes were on Star as she climbed up on the sausage podium.

'STAR HAS SHOWN MANY QUALITIES. SHE HAS SPEED AND AGILITY. BUT SHE HAS SOMETHING ELSE TOO: BRAVERY AND TRUE LOYALTY IN THE FACE OF DANGER. THE MOUNTAIN RESCUE TEAM SAID THEY HAD

NEVER SEEN SUCH BRAVERY
BEFORE, AND THEY HAVE
AWARDED STAR THE HIGHEST
HONOUR, THE MUNRO MEDAL.'

Angus stepped forward to put the
medal around Star's neck.

Everyone cheered. Professor
Offenbach had to wave her paws to
quieten everyone down.

'AND,' she continued, 'THEY
HAVE ASKED IF STAR WOULD
CONSIDER TRAINING TO BE
PART OF THEIR TEAM. THEY
THINK SHE WILL BE THE PERFECT
MOUNTAIN RESCUE DOG.'

Star could hardly believe
her ears. She could do

something where she could run and run and run across the mountains and feel the wild wind in her fur. Star was standing on the sausage podium, but she felt as if she were standing on the very top of the world.

Professor Offenbach turned to Star. '**WHAT DO YOU THINK, STAR? DO YOU WANT TO BE A MOUNTAIN RESCUE DOG ONE DAY?**'

'WOOF!' agreed Star. 'WOOF! WOOF! WOOF!'

'**AND JUST ONE THING MORE,**' said Professor Offenbach, beckoning the old Herdwick ewe onto the stage.

The old ewe climbed up and faced
Star. 'The girls and I wanted to say
thank you for saving one of our little
lambs. We got together and made
you a little present.' She held up a
woollen coat. 'Made out of the finest
Herdwick wool,' she bleated. 'It's the
warmest wool in the whole world.
It'll keep you warm and dry out on
any mountain.'

'Thank you,' said Star, beaming. 'Thank you.'

Those Herdwick sheep weren't so scary after all.

After the ceremony, Star went to find some peace and quiet in the barn.

She lay down in the straw next to Hilda and Mabel.

'Oooh! It suits you,' bleated Hilda, admiring the Herdwick coat.

'Suits you,' baa-ed Mabel. 'Lovely bit of cable knit that.'

'Star?'

Star looked up. Her mum had found her.

'I'm sorry,' said Star.

Star's mum sat down next to her. 'Sorry for what?'

Star stared at her own paws. 'I know we come from a long line of sheepdogs, but that's not what I want to be. I want to be a mountain rescue dog. I hope I can make you proud of me.'

Lillabelle put her paw on Star. 'I have never been more proud of you than I am today. What you did on the mountain was very, very brave. But it doesn't matter what you do or how well you do it. I just love you as you.'

Star looked up at her mum.

'Really?'

'Really!' smiled Lillabelle, giving her a kiss. 'Star, my little pup, you'll always be a champion to me.'

MORE PUPPY ACADEMY STORIES COMING SOON!

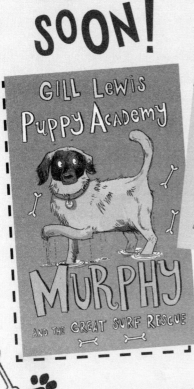

Meet Fern, a Real Life Search and Rescue Dog!

Name
Fern

Age
9

Occupation
Search and rescue dog

Likes
Tennis ball games,
'Cheesy Bites' snacks

Hates
Cats!

Fern uses her nose to search for missing people, and lets her handler know that she has found someone by barking.

Mission Statement

NSARDA is a charity supporting the training of Search and Rescue dogs. These dogs help find missing people in mountains, towns, parks and in water. NSARDA dogs and handlers belong to Search and Rescue teams, and work all over the UK.

Registration number 1069110
Find out more at www.nsarda.org.uk

National Search And Rescue Dog Association · NSARDA ·

SEARCH AND RESCUE DOG FACTS!

Search and rescue dogs use their noses to find human scent, but their amazing sense of hearing and their ability to see in the dark can also help.

DID YOU KNOW?

It is thought that a single dog can accomplish the work of 20–30 human searchers.

Mountain rescue dogs like Star are air-scenting dogs. They pick up a scent on the air, and follow it to its source.

DID YOU KNOW?

Rescue dogs who travel in helicopters, like Snowdon in the story, have to have flight training!

Border collies like Star make great search and rescue dogs, but German shepherds, labradors and spaniels are also popular.

DID YOU KNOW?

One of the earliest-known mountain rescue dogs was a St Bernard, called Barry. He worked in Switzerland in the early 1800s and saved more than 40 lives.

ABOUT NED AND HIS OWNER, GILL LEWIS

I'm **NED**, a Border collie just like Star. My mum was a champion sheepdog too. I was born on a farm in Devon with seven brothers and sisters before I went to live with **GILL LEWIS** and her family. She doesn't have any sheep, but she does have chickens and so I love rounding those up instead. I love playing ball and Frisbee.

My feet never stop. I'm always running, running, and running. I always need a job to do. If no one wants to play with me, I play with my best friend Murphy, a Leonberger. He even puts up with me when I pull his tail. You might meet him in some of the other Puppy Academy books. You'll have to excuse me, I can't hang around here talking ... I've got to run ...

Here are some other stories we think you'll love ...